Spirits Unveiled

Courtney Pellegrino

Dedication

Salem, 1692. We will never forget you.

Acknowledgment

Dad, thank you for always loving and believing in me and my gifts. Without you, none of this would have evolved.Laurie Cabot and my entire Cabot family of Salem and New Orleans, thank you for your unwavering love, support, and guidance throughout my journey from childhood.To my husband and children, thank you for always keeping me grounded through your love and jokes.To my best friend, Julie. Thank you for always providing love, laughter, and insight. Thank you for breaking that glass.

Table of Contents

v

About the Author

Dr. Courtney Pellegrino is a third-generation psychic medium. She holds four graduate degrees, including a Master's degree in Special Education, an Education Specialist, and two doctoral degrees: Ed.D. (Northeastern) and a Ph.D. in Metaphysical Humanistic Science. When she is not writing, doing readings, or working on cases, Courtney can be found running, at the beach, or spending time with her husband and children.

Page Blank Intentionally

Chapter 1

Meeting new people was always an awkward experience for me. It started with an exchange of pleasantries and names, and then came the question, "So what do you do for work?"

I explained, "I am a forensic psychic medium and what that entail. I will know within the first 5 seconds if they will be a friend, or if they are running for the hills."

As a third-generation psychic medium and witch, I was born with the ability to read energy to determine past, present, and future events and communicate with the dead.

When I was three, my mother wanted to take me to see my first movie in the theatre, "Mary Poppins." Weeks later, a spirit woman in my bedroom started to appear. She would come and go through my closet. She looked like Mary Poppins in her long but not as colorful black and tan outfit, but her face was different. The clothes resembled more of a servant from the Victorian period. This woman was calm and patient with me, she would sit with me while I played in my room, but never anywhere else in the home. I am not sure if she was a spirit or a guide. She also encouraged me during my naptime to put on my tap shoes and tap on my closet floor, which was wooden. She was kind enough to move the clothes out of the way onto the floor, all of them still on hangers. I remember my father rushing in to see what was happening. Interestingly, he checked the closet even though

"

I did not tell him about my spirit friend. I just sat on my bed, swinging my four-year-old legs and smiling while he tried to figure out what just happened there. She stood behind him and said, "Shh," before she went back into the closet.

The rest of the house was active as well but not in an always pleasant way. I would often play with my toys by myself in that basement. There was one area I never wanted to go near. It was inside the basement, a separate room for the washer and dryer. Past that was an area that alarmed me even more. I tried not to go near that if I could ever avoid it. There was a brick wall with a strange opening, like an alcove for a stove or fire pit on the wall. I always got chills and feelings of dread in that area. My Mom had to do laundry and wanted company, I talked to her from the other room. That is how it started her famous Mom saying, "I'm not having a long-distance conversation over here." Anytime I had to go downstairs and get cat food near that door, I would run, grab the food, and race back up the stairs as fast as my little legs could carry me. The door had a chain on it from the outside, so the cat could go up and down as needed. One day, I went down to get cat food. I saw someone standing at the bottom of the stairs behind me, one hand on the railing. I screamed and ran upstairs as fast as I could, slamming the door behind me.

There was another occasion in the basement, but I was much older. I have just received a radio with a tape recorder. It was important in those days. I recorded a rock song off the radio in the basement. When I played it back, I heard a man call "Courtney!" a split second before the chorus. I always thought it was so cool my name was in the song. When I heard it on the radio the next time, I tried to hear my name, but it wasn't there. For almost 30 years, every time I listened to that song on a CD or radio, I waited for that part. It was never there. Recently, I finally realized that it was an EVP of a spirit saying my name in the basement. In fact, as I was writing this, I pulled the song up on my phone to check again. Nope. No "Courtney!"

My maternal grandparents were such an important part of my life, and still are. I spent most of my life with them. My Grandpa Joe was a pivotal part of my life. Although I was truly spoiled rotten by him, the most precious gift he gave me was his time and a listening ear. He truly was my best friend, protector, and advocate. He always listened to all my childish fantasies, hopes, and dreams. He once gave me sage advice. Grandpa Joe always told me, "Never settle for anything in life, Princess. Not men, friends, jobs, nothing."

I have carried that advice with me my entire life.

Grandpa always listened to what I shared about my visions of the future and the spirits I was communicating without judgment. One teenage spirit named Tommy often showed up. He had blond curly hair, and it was styled in what I would describe as the longer seventies style. He wore a yellow T-shirt and jeans. He usually showed up when I was either with him or my mother, but neither seemed to know who he was. Grandpa Joe was notorious for buying unusual vehicles with no rhyme or reason, other than it sparked his interest. The one that really made Grandma the maddest was the small school bus. He parked it on the side of the driveway, and I would play in there for hours (no keys, obviously). As the "bus driver," Tommy would be right there playing along with me. He made sure I was never alone. He also served as a protector and would often alert my grandfather if something was wrong. I spent the night at Grandma and Grandpa's house. I woke up the next morning, and Grandma was still sleeping. It was about six in the morning. I went into the kitchen to get myself cereal, which involved climbing. I was ridiculously small for my age and was like a monkey scampering up counters. However, this time, I fell, and I landed on an open cabinet door. I was stuck. I was crying, in pain, and scared as there was no feasible way to get down due to my short legs. Grandma slept through it because she could sleep through a hurricane. Tommy was there but had a helpless look on his face.

"Tommy, help me!" I cried.

There was no response from snoring Grandma, but a few minutes later, Grandpa came flying in the door. He had gone out to get his morning coffee. He had planned to stop for more cigarettes but instead got a weird warning to come home right away. Tommy warned him, and I thanked him for that. I did not see Tommy anymore after we moved to Virginia. He figured I did not need him anymore.

Grandma Rosie was a true matriarch and guiding force of our family. She loved to create with her hands, doing ceramics and painting. This creativity was passed down to my cousin Deborah, who is extremely gifted in ceramics and creating jewelry. Grandma passed over when she was in her nineties. At her funeral viewing services, I observed her standing over by the coat rack by the front entrance. She told me she was watching to see who showed up, and then she would go from there. She was pleased with who came, especially my father's work friends. That meant the world to her to have recognition and honor for her place in this world. That is really what the spirit world wants: recognition.

From what my spirit guides and the spirit world have shown me, the afterlife is more of a separate but parallel dimension. As I stated before, energy does not die, and it must land somewhere. My Grandma Rosie became very intertwined with this dimension over the course of several events through the years. She has made her presence known, like she did during her life. The first Easter after she passed, we were having dinner around the dining room table at my parent's home. There was plenty of food on the table, as always. It was a strange feeling not having her there as her voice was usually the loudest of the din. As we started talking, the chandelier lights began to flicker. They dimmed then rose, dimmed then rose.

"Ok, Grandma! You can stop now. We know you are here!" She stopped, but we made sure to address her in conversation after that. Months later, my mother was vacuuming the living room to prepare for family dinners. The vacuum would unplug by itself. Grandma would do this for years to come. Grandpa Joe would sit in the living room in his special spot, even after he crossed over. His presence was so tangible, you could smell his scent of Old Spice on the chair till the end of the night.

Great Grandma Amelia (Amena was her real name) was a powerful force of a Bohemian Romani Gypsy immigrant woman. Amelia came to the United States and worked as a servant for a wealthy New York City Jewish family, from whom she learned Yiddish. After she married Grandpa Edward (also Bohemian Romani), she was a well-respected psychic reader and medium in her New York neighborhood. She was consulted by many prominent members to consult on community matters with notable members. When I was little, I loved to visit her in the nursing home. I was about 3 or 4 years old. She always called me "Little Rosie," and anytime I wanted to say something, she would listen intently. I remember her giving me ice cream cups and her deck of playing cards. She would throw them on a tray table in a tarot spread and do her psychic readings. One day, I imitated her tarot throw, and Grandma Rosie cried out, "Oh No!" Amelia held up her hand to my grandmother. She replied in a strong Bohemian accent that did not allow for a /l/ pronunciation, "Vet her, Rosie. Vet's see what she does." I sorted the cards into piles, cut the deck, and then created a story with the pictures I saw in my mind. My body felt completely charged with electricity and excitement. I connected immediately to my sense of the other world. I threw a tantrum when it was time to leave her and go home. I would hang onto Amelia and cry, "No!" and she would smirk at Grandma Rosie. That was my first and last tarot throw for the next 10 years. I did not receive my tarot deck until much later, when I was sixteen in Salem, but I remembered what Great Grandma showed me.

Grandma Rosie had a small upstairs storage space in her home. Grandma Rosie kept photos and other treasures in there, including a beautifully painted wedding portrait of Amelia and her husband, Edward. I preferred to play for hours and hours by myself up there. Little did the family know that the reason I would spend time up there was to hang out and converse with my great-grandfather Edward (who had been dead for decades). After Amelia passed over at the age of ninety-nine, she appeared in the attic as well. I do remember them speaking in a different language to each other, which I know now was Bohemian Romani. I just learned the inappropriate words from Grandma Rosie. As a child, sitting up there and just listening to them, playing with my toys and a deck of playing cards.

Overall, the love and support from my father and paternal grandparents facilitated my growth and safety within the spirit world and my gifts. My family was constantly trying to find ways to support my development in a safe and effective manner by bringing me to the experts in the metaphysical. We often visited Sturbridge village and Salem village. Salem was very different in the 1980s and 90s. I felt most at home when I was there, wandering the cobblestone streets and eating dinner on the Pickering Wharf. We would shop, dine out, and connect with other witches. The older I became, the more the trips increased.

Since my gifts were so encouraged at home, I often felt confident sharing my abilities with others. However, not all sides of my family were as supportive. My mother once shared that her parents said I was "strange and had odd ways about me." The visions and messages that I shared were not welcomed. I barely saw them once a year and that was good enough for me. The day that my maternal grandmother died, I was sitting in a summer school math class and daydreaming about other things: clothes and boys. The daydreaming and avoidance of math were quite suddenly interrupted. The maternal grandmother showed up in my presence. I knew immediately she had crossed over, and I started to wonder if I would inherit the large TV they owned in their living room. Hey, I was a teenager without a TV, mind you! That afternoon, my mother picked me up from school, crying. She shared that her mother had passed away that morning and that we would need to pack for the trip to Pennsylvania. I felt no sadness since I did not have any relationship with my maternal grandparents. Plus, I was excited because Grandma Rosie was coming with us on the trip!

After the funeral, my mother and I lived in Scranton on and off while we settled the estate and prepared the home for sale. Grandma Rosie would sometimes accompany us on our trips, and it was a comfort to have her there. Those school breaks and summers were some of the best times of my life. The house itself was pleasant. I never felt comfortable visiting there when the grandparents were alive, but afterwards it felt more open and more like our space. Settled in the inner city of Scranton, we had sidewalks that ran between the homes. These were also cut-throughs for the neighborhood kids. The back porch led to the backyard, which was a simple grass patch with a tiny herb garden. The backdrop to our yard was the neighborhood clotheslines that ran through all the yards and connected to apartments. We spent most of our time with the next-door neighbors. Since I was a small child, the neighbors have become more like my family than my actual grandparents. Although our house was nice, their home was beautiful. It was filled with love, laughter, and acceptance. I cannot count how many nights Mom and I would go over to their house and not leave until after eleven, often topping off the night with a delivered pizza as a "snack." The laughter from those nights has stayed with me throughout my life.

A very strong favorite memory of them was when I was about four or five. I visited our neighbors and talked to Louise's husband in the living room as we all sat around chatting and enjoying the holiday treats. I was surprised when he didn't give me money or candy, as he usually gave me a dollar when I came over. I continued to talk with him and was confused when later, his daughters were discussing the funeral procedures, including putting pictures and coins in his pockets. I then realized he had transitioned to the other side.

Our own Scranton house had a strange energy to it, often when I least expected it. I could still feel the presence of my mother's parents there, watching us and living their daily routines around ours. My mother did not smoke, and I never smoked on the property. My paternal grandparents were avid smokers, and I would often smell fresh cigarette smoke wafting in and out of the kitchen, along with a whiff of my grandma's perfume now and then. I would close the kitchen cabinet doors, only to come back into the room and find one or two open again. Once we traveled back to Virginia, we knew the house would be watched by Louise and her beautiful daughters. Mom and I made sure anything that was a potential fire or electrical hazard was unplugged. We would get calls from neighbors about noise disturbances at night coming from the home, including the stove timer alarm (which could ironically wake the dead if it was that loud) going off all hours of the night. The stove had been unplugged, making that impossible. The unplugged upstairs antique phone would ring all hours of the night.

On our next trip up, I decided to sleep in my grandmother's room. I wanted independence as a teenager and my own space. One morning, I woke up to see her spirit standing next to my bed and touching my arm. I yelled, and after that, I slept in the same room as my Mom. Despite a lack of emotional connection or relationship with those grandparents, they did appear every now and then during dreams to deliver messages. They always appeared in the home, sometimes waving at the front door.

When I turned sixteen years old, Grandma Rosie gave me her engagement ring. It was not your typical ring. This ring was an almost pink amethyst with two tiny diamonds on both sides. Grandma's side of the family has a strong connection to amethysts and their healing powers. A year later, I had cookie mix on my hands while baking. I went into the bathroom to wash my hands. I forgot to put it back on. The next morning, as I put my rings on, I remembered the ring. I ran back into the bathroom, and my heart sank when I realized it was gone. I did not dare tell Grandma Rosie! It meant the world to me, and I was visibly upset. My mother lectured me about taking better care of my things. I asked her to please help me find it. I looked everywhere: under couches, drawers, even outside. I could not locate it. I went to bed upset and prayed to the Goddess that I would find it before Grandma Rosie found out.

Later that night, I dreamed my other grandmother and I were in the bedroom in Scranton. She was helping me look through her vanity table drawers, but we could not find it. She turned to me and said, "Your mother has it." I woke up.

I was busy the next day with work and did not have a chance to tell my Mom about the dream. That night, I came home from work. I could hear the spirits whispering in my ear, "Ask her." My mother was preparing dinner for a larger family gathering.

I walked over to the island counter and questioned, "Do you have my ring?"

She asked why I would ever think that.

I calmly said, "Your mother told me last night."

She turned pale, stopped making dinner, and got the ring. She placed it in her own jewelry box to keep it safe and teach me a lesson about taking better care of my things. I realized then that dreams were a way for the spirit world to connect with me and often give me messages to help myself and others. Sometimes giving me more than I bargained for!

During my high school years, I became friends with a family of Romani readers who lived close to my home. I received a reading from the great aunt one night when I visited the family. The reading was spot on, and she shared that I would dump him, communicate with the other side, get married, have two boys, and become a writer. I shared the reading with the guy I was dating then. He proclaimed that was witchcraft and that I should pray, or I would go to hell. I did not share the rest of the reading…or my gifts. It was not the time to share that I also did readings, for payment as well. I had to hide who I was for the relationship to survive.

This set the tone for the recurring theme of my dating life: hide and survive.

Chapter 2
True To My Nature

College was a period of painful growth and transition. I was on my own for the first time in my life, never having even been to a sleepover camp. It was a difficult adjustment, to say the least. I found myself trying too hard to avoid my gifts and fit in. I had a few friends, but few knew the real me. Looking back, I wish I had connected more to the other side rather than the living. It would have saved me a ton of heartache. No one knew the real me- the authentic self that could read energy and communicate with the dead. I felt like I was wearing a mask, most of the time to fit in. I was far away from my family and in survival mode.

During my freshman year, I lived in a haunted dorm hall. It was a lovely building with strict rules for female first-year students. The legend was that a female student had hung herself upstairs in a separate attic/room area. The dorm Resident Assistants insisted there was nothing up there. She took a group of us up there, stood outside the door, and said, "See, there's nothing here." I hung back, as I did not want to get near that door. She never opened the door, and we went back downstairs. Many of the girls were disappointed, but I just wanted to get away from that area. Months later, I was alone in my room watching a vampire movie. The movie ended, and I turned the TV off. I stood up and stretched. As I turned back around, I realized I was not alone. In the reflection of the dark TV screen, a girl was standing behind me. I turned around as fast as I could, but no one was there. Terrified, I ran out of the room and went to stay in a friend's room that night. As I reflect as an adult, I wish I had asked who she was and what she wanted, but at that moment, I was out of there like a bat out of hell. I watched that movie hundreds of times after that (I like predictability) and not once after I turned off the TV did it occur again.

That summer I returned home to Virginia. My father's dear witch and medium friend came to see me, as my dad felt I needed a little mentoring. She asked why I was pushing my true self down so much. I shared that I did not want to be different at college, and I wanted to be "just like everyone else." She looked at me and said, "You are not like everyone else. You are like me, and we are special. Stop trying to be something you are not: mundane."

I wasn't sure whether I wanted to return to college in Missouri. I was homesick for my family but knew that my place wasn't in Virginia anymore. This was an even stickier situation since I had met someone. As fate would have it, Grandma Rosie was over the house one night. My parents were away on a trip. Grandma and I went out to dinner. As much as I can talk with Grandma as a medium now, I would give about anything to just hold her hand and have another dinner with her, gathering her advice. She asked me what I was going to do (about leaving). I knew in my heart what I needed to do, and she did, too. Going back to Missouri would change everything. I would be on a different course once again, other than the life I created that summer for myself. I told her that I honestly did not know what to do. We got into the house, and she said, "Someone's calling." The phone had not rung. About 2 minutes later, the phone rang. I answered and it was the Missouri University provost, asking what I decided about returning. I told her I needed to think about it. I got off the phone, and Grandma stared me down.

"Well, what's it going to be?" At that moment, it came out. "I am going back. I do not belong here."

"Well, that is what you do. And listen, missy. You'd better buckle down and stop all that partying." She was correct, but I do need to add that wise old Grandma Rosie was a flapper in the late 1920's, and I now know what exactly that and a speakeasy means, Grandma.

She knew exactly what I was going to do before I did, but in that moment, I had free will. We always do. I could have chosen to stay, and my life would have taken quite a different path. Not better or worse, but different. I returned to Missouri, knowing that was where I needed to be. Although I did not know exactly why at the time.

I returned to college and lived in the dorms again. It was months later that I had a particularly vivid and terrifying dream. I dreamed that in the middle of the night, a little girl between eight and eleven years old showed up naked and dirty in my room. She was crying and terrified. The girl was shaking with fear.

"You must hide me!"

I said, "Oh my God! Who? Who is trying to hurt you? Here! Let me get you some clothes! What happened?"

"He is going to hurt me. He cannot find me!" I said, "Ok, but let's get you dressed first- I have clothes you can borrow." As she climbed into the closet, I still remember the sound of the sliding door closing on its own. The dream continued. I left the room, went to a college party, and forgot about her. When I got back to the room, I saw the closet, remembered, and cried out. I was frantically trying to find her, to get her help. I woke up crying out, "I forgot to get her help!" I never shared that dream with anyone until almost thirty years later when I realized who she might be. I now know she was the victim of a serial killer.

The spirit world was trying to get my attention at that point, but I kept fighting it. I wanted to be a regular college girl. I wanted to worry about what I was going to wear to a party that night, not having dead people showing up to chat or seek help from me. Anything that made me seem weird or not included, I avoided those conversations. Yet, a huge part of me was missing. We returned to Salem for a trip. While eating a lobster dinner at Victoria Station on Pickering Wharf, I commented that I could eat lobster every day of my life.

My father joked, "You'd better marry someone

wealthy!"

I replied, "Nope, I am going to marry a boy from Boston, so I can have lobster anytime I want!"

Little did I know that was to come to fruition.

The rest of my college years were spent preparing for my career as a teacher. I worked at a college daycare. I graduated and secured a job teaching Head Start and later as a Special Education teacher. At this point, I limited my interactions with the spirit world for a few years and ignored signs from them. The changing point came for me when I worked for Head Start and met two beautiful friends: Jan and Tami. Much to my surprise, Jan was like me. She came from a lengthy line of witches, shamans, readers, and healers. We would meet up and practice spellwork and readings.

However, not everyone in my life was a huge supporter of my practice and gifts. I joined a witch and spirit class at the local shop. It was so close to my house; I could have walked there. The first class was in a hidden backroom of the shop, which had a mysterious and magical aura to it. It was as if when we were back there, that section of the building was invisible to the rest of the world. The owner began the class with a brief history of the persecutions we faced as witches in most countries across the world. She asked if anyone was familiar with Salem. I raised my hand, and she asked me to share what I knew. It was just a brief statement about the hysteria, dates, and innocence that were hung, but in that moment, I was completely empowered. We practiced meditation and visualization spells to strengthen our abilities and connections to the other side. I left that class on a complete spiritual high and a renewed vow to continue my work. That came crashing down when I shared it with my then-boyfriend. He insisted I drop out because he felt it was taking too much of his time. The class was held for one day a week for two hours. I wound up dropping out of the development class there due to my then boyfriend's distaste for it. To this very day, I wish I had not. I remember the conversation I had when I went in to drop the class. The owner tried to convince me to stay. She implored me to really think it over and not base my decision on one person.

"There will always be people that will try to turn you away from it. Stay true to yourself, and true to your nature." As an impressionable twenty-year-old who thought they were in love and desperate to please others, I dropped the class, and she refunded my $20. As she handed me the money, she foretold, "I think you are making a big mistake." To this very day, I wish I had listened to her. The relationship ended shortly after. I went back to the store to register for the class again. To my disappointment, the shop had closed. However, the lesson learned stayed with me. I should not have forced down my nature. At the very least, I should have kept going with my training, but I did not. I had the fear of the witch hunt in me.

I moved back to Virginia in the early 2000s and quickly

met my husband. The Boston boy I predicted years before that I would marry. Time marched on, and we had two amazing sons. During the births of my sons, the spirit world showed up in the delivery room. My first son's labor was twenty-three hours long. By the time the delivery rolled around, the epidural had worn off. The delivery was rough, and I was having a tough time getting him to move. My husband was on the right, holding my leg, and a blonde nurse was holding my left leg. I remember her grabbing my arm and squeezing it to give encouragement. As I gave the final push, the pain was so intense that I screamed and ran my nails down that nurse's arm so hard. As I sank back into the pillows and started to close my eyes, I saw Grandpa Joe standing by me. I was sure that I had just crossed over. After about an hour, the nurse came in to check on me and the baby. I asked about the nurse. I felt so badly that I had hurt her. When I described her, the nurse had no idea about whom I was talking. She stated that no one was on my left, and only my husband was on my right. They were so short-staffed that night due to the full moon. That angel or spirit guide has shown up repeatedly for my oldest son.

A year later, my best friend Tami crossed over to heaven very unexpectedly. I was never able to say goodbye, as I found out about her passing a month later. She still found ways to connect with me every so often. She would play with my hair when I would rock my youngest son to sleep in his room. After she crossed over, I received a phone call, but I let the answering machine pick up as I was upstairs, putting my oldest son down for bedtime. I heard her voice on the machine saying, "Hello, hello?" I grabbed my son and ran down the stairs as fast as I safely could. There was no known number on the cordless phone- just "unknown" and no recording.

Not long after that, my cell phone went off in the middle of the night. It was her phone number popping up. I figured it was her daughter calling and let it go to voicemail due to it being 1in the morning. I figured I would talk to her the next day. When I called her, she was very confused and shared that the cell phone number had been shut off right after her mother's death, so that was impossible.

I dreamed about Tami several times. One time, we were both on a boat. The water had waves, but it did not rock the boat at all. I asked her where she was. Tami smiled and said, "I cannot even describe where I am. I cannot show you, but I am so happy."

These dreams were a way to reach out. I often tell clients that when loved ones come through, it is indeed them trying to connect. I have experienced through my spirit interactions that if they are happy and look healthy, it is them. If they appear ill or injured, it is not them. That is just your consciousness recreating them in your mind's story. When the spirit world wants to communicate, they can be relentless. Messages can come through at any time and any place, but it is imperative to listen. It is my most heartfelt advice to believe in your visions when you see them. It is extremely easy to doubt yourself, especially if someone tells you it is just your imagination. I think the worst thing I was ever told was that my gifts were not from a higher power but something evil and more sinister. I am very thankful I did not listen, as many times it has saved a life.

My triggers for visions and spirit interactions can be anything and occur anywhere for me. Years ago, I was at swimming lessons with my two sons. As they were playing water games and working on stroke skills, I watched the mothers and their infants in the water. I smiled and reminisced about when the boys were that age. That was the trigger for me, and I was overtaken by a vision where I saw myself diving into that very pool, fully clothed, to save a child. It felt so real that I was having trouble breathing. I figured I was being oversensitive to the babies. Four days later, it happened. We were at a pool party. Due to the vision, I refused to leave the poolside to use the bathroom or even chat with the other parents. Thirty minutes into the party, my son started to tread water, he went down and up, and then down again. The second time he came up, he had a strange look on his face. As he went under again, I dove into that pool, fully clothed, to save him. He was drowning, and there was a woman holding a baby next to him, not even realizing what was happening beside her. I beat the lifeguard to get to him. I do not even remember jumping out of the flip-flops, but I did. A dad realized what happened as I swam with my son, met me at the poolside, and pulled him out, then me. The rest of the party was too distracted to even realize what was happening. The details still infuriate me, but I thank God every day for my gifts and the many second chances they have afforded my family, friends, and clients.

A few years ago, I was reading for a lovely woman. Her energy was so bright and open. She wanted to know more about her current relationship. She had been on a few dates with this man and wanted to see what he thought of her. I smiled and started to tap into that energy. Without warning, my body and energy were completely assaulted with nausea and fear. I had the vision of her being assaulted physically and possibly dying. I saw this man had a hidden temper that emerged as a dark side of himself and had given slight hints of this before with other women, but not to this level as it would be with her. She was upset, and I begged her to please warn others when she would be traveling with him, particularly out of town or state. She agreed. Months later, she emailed and validated the reading as he had flown off the handle about something trivial, and she ended the relationship, remembering my warning.

As the years have grown, so has the ability for spirits to physically affect me. I have been poked, touched, scratched, punched, shocked, and choked. I sometimes become nauseated and have a backache and headache. I will often have tingles running up and down my body, like electrical currents. I often wonder why I am now more physically sensitive to them now than when I was a child. The only thing I can think of was that when I was a child and teen, my brain and body believed they were natural events to communicate with the spirit world. As I have aged, my mind often fights about what is happening. As an amazing medium once shared with me that I am human but what I do is not human. I have learned to control many aspects of the physical elements by grounding before, during, and after readings. However, it is not always foolproof. I am not always able to clear as quickly as I like.

As I mentioned earlier, I often work missing and cold person cases for families and law enforcement personnel across the United States. One cold case hit a little too close to home. I was participating in a Psychic Detective Zoom class to hone my skills in remote viewing. The instructor was a gifted psychic medium who has worked on many cases over the years, bringing justice and closure to victims and families. One of the assignments was for us to remote view. According to the instructor, remote viewing is when you perceive details about a location, event, or object without being physically present, relying on psychic or intuitive means instead." Anything they can show you may help the case. We are often given only a name, or a picture, or a location, which is it. The task was for us to be shown a picture and no further info. The instructor held up a picture of a young girl. I immediately got a warning buzz. I shared that I thought I knew who it was because although the picture was not familiar to me, the girl's energy was. The other medium started that remote view. For my task, I was shown a man in an older picture. I immediately went into the view too fast. I was shown he was walking down an office hallway towards a parking garage. He got into the car and was in the driver's seat when his life ended. I was also shown that, connected to the event, he was punched in the left arm by a female. I also saw heartburn medicine in the car. I asked Spirit to show me further details as I was starting to feel nauseous and connected to this man. They showed me two highway signs: "Welcome to Myrtle Beach, South Carolina" and "Welcome to Virginia." I came out and relayed this to the instructor.

She said, "Well done, thank you."

She then moved to the next picture. It was a girl I had gone to high school with who was part of a serial murder case in my former hometown. I had just remote-viewed a serial killer. I was visibly shaken, and the instructor encouraged me to take a break.

The class continued on the rest of the case, including the other female child victims. I returned to the class to share why I reacted. After the class, the instructor reached out. I told her I would call the next day. I went outside and cried. My husband came to check on me, and I shared what had happened. He said, "I don't know what to do?" He just held me as I cried about how I was starting to feel like I could not control any of this. As he stroked my back, he said, "I thought you were normal when I met you."

"No, there were signs." I choked out, and we both laughed.

Once I calmed down, I called my dad and described the situation to him. I felt calmer at this point, knowing my father had seen some horrific crime scenes and profiled horrible monsters. He assured me that my skills would help others and that he wished he had someone like me to help when he was working on his cases. I finally shared with him the dream I had about the young naked girl in my college room. He and I both felt that she was one of the killer's victims.

When I later spoke with the instructor, I shared my connection to the case. The one victim went to high school with me, although she was a few years behind me. We did not know each other well, but we parked our cars close together and would say hi every day. My mother worked at two of the victims' elementary schools. The girl who escaped the killer later became a police officer. She gave a presentation to my husband's unit when he was in the force. There were too many connections, but the worst part was the sheer terror I felt after I remotely viewed the killer. It was such a horrific feeling to view what they viewed. We spoke about the ability to see events and people we cannot physically send help to, but we can send our energy instead. It took days of diving into a saltwater swimming pool and crying to release that energy. As my instructor said, it was not mine to keep.

Children's cases are the toughest for me. There was a homicide case involving a young girl in New England. I had not paid attention to it because I never watched the news. One Saturday, my husband had the local news station on. They were showing the search for any evidence related to her murder. I knew I could not connect to her spirit as it was too much for me as a mother. I knew nothing of the case, as I never watched the news anyway. I got in the car, and as I was driving about 20 minutes later, her spirit showed up. She could not understand why they could not find her. I tried to stay calm as I was driving a car and assured her that the police and multiple agencies were searching for her as hard as they could. I told her that there would be dogs out and for her to do whatever she could to get the police officer's attention.

"Trip them. You must make them see where your stuff is."

She kept showing me a sign for a city about an hour from where we were. I called the local detective and left a message. They called back and asked for further details, which I gave. It was months later, but an arrest was finally made based on the information I gave.

Chapter 3
The Magic Of New England

We moved to New England in 2020, in the middle of the world shutting down. Although we settled in New Hampshire, my family and I spent most of our time in Massachusetts.

Salem, Massachusetts, is a town filled with love and magic, darkness, and hope. Although it has a horrific past stemming from the Salem Witch trials, there is resilience observed in a few other places.

I am a firm believer in the magical properties of Salem, Massachusetts. It is not only connected to the vast history of the area but also to the current residents as well. When I was 21 years old, I accidentally dropped a silver wave ring into Pickering Wharf while looking at the boats. Twenty years later, my youngest son and husband were metal detecting on a New Hampshire beach. That evening, I walked into my son's bedroom. I saw a ring on the floor and picked it up. I put it on in shock.

I said to my husband, "Where did you find this?"

He said, "We found it metal detecting today. It is a perfect fit!" gesturing to the ring on my finger. "That's because it's mine!" It was the same ring I had lost 20 years beforehand.

My youngest son and I were visiting Witch City. We decided to go to Witch House. Although I had not been there in many years, my youngest son wanted to go. We walked in, and immediately as we walked upstairs, I saw a Black woman walking up the stairs, carrying a large basket of clothes. She was beautiful, pregnant. She glanced back at me and gave me a look. I followed her up. When we got to the top of the stairs, I stood at the desk with my son. I felt someone brushing against my leg. I started to ask the person to move, as we were under strict COVID measures then. When I turned to say something, no one was there. There were no other people upstairs. Well, living, that is.

A few months later, we decided to eat at a popular pizza place in Salem. We had never eaten there before, and my sons kept fighting me on it. I insisted upon it. We always ate at the fabulous Red's Sandwich Shop, and I wanted to be adventurous and try something new. We had about half an hour until our reservations, so we decided to use the bathroom before heading back onto Essex Street. As soon as I crossed into the hallway where the bathrooms were, I could feel a horrible shift between this world and the other. My youngest son stated that he did not like it there. He could feel someone watching us in the hallway next to the bathrooms. I could feel the same presence but felt that someone or something in that area of the building had either opened a portal or prolonged one. I assured my son that everything was okay. He went into one bathroom, and I went into the other. When I sat down to use the bathroom, a pair of shadow legs walked across in front of my own legs. I was terrified and felt completely violated. I looked up to see if there was a light source from above, but there was not. The ceiling was completely closed off, with no possibility of light coming from above. I checked in with another Salem witch about my experiences. She informed me that the site where the pizza place was located where Martha Corey was originally examined for evidence of witchcraft on that exact date during the Salem Witch trials.

Once I moved to New England, I felt more comfortable about being open and doing events. My father encouraged me to pursue further training from Laurie Cabot, the High Priestess of the Cabot Kent Hermetic Temple. During my training with her, my gifts evolved to the point where I felt more in control. During psychic and mediumship readings for clients, it is my hope that can deliver the messages from Spirit as well as connect them with loved ones. I use a variety of methods to engage with the spirit world- tarot cards, crystals, and automatic writing. I do not require them, but it gives me an anchor between something tangible and the other side. I used to light a candle before all readings, but many event venues forbade it due to fire hazards. I now envelop myself with light and spiritual protection prior to the reading. I prefer to close my eyes when reading, as it keeps me connected to the spirit world and not focus on how the sitter is reacting.

My experiences with the spirit world were not limited to Massachusetts. Going to work could be a paranormal event as well. My position allowed me to work in five different elementary schools. The important thing to note is that these schools date back to the 1800s, with their original but well-maintained structures. A co-worker gave me and the other new educators a tour of the one school during my first week. We walked outside to get some air, as the school was not air-conditioned. As we were talking, I felt an overwhelming amount of pressure on my chest. It got to the point where I thought I was having an asthma attack. I kept looking over to the empty grass area. She saw me looking and commented to another teacher how she remembered when a child had tragically passed on the property due to a trauma to his chest.

My best friend Julie (also a witch and medium) would be sitting in her office and immediately start "pinging" off each other with the dead. It did not matter where we were.

One day, I was sitting in her office as we were having an early lunch. Julie was talking about her husband's father on the other side. All of a sudden, a male spirit put immense pressure on my back, like he was trying to push through me to get to Julie.

Noticing my expression, she stopped talking and said, "Are you okay? You look like you are about the cry."

"No, Julie. I am about to throw up."

I told her what happened, and she immediately

connected with the spirit it was her loved one who had recently crossed over, Michael.

Cemeteries are also a favorite "haunt" of mine. I enjoy running, walking, and exploring them. In New Hampshire, my oldest son and I planned to investigate this haunted resting area: the Gilson Cemetery. I was a little bit disappointed when I saw how small and damaged it was, with six stones visible from the road. We had driven over 40 minutes to get here! My son was so excited to finally be a part of his first paranormal investigation. I observed the deteriorated gate swing back and forth despite the fact there was no wind that day. I parked the car and directed my son to wait until I exited the car, as it was a terribly busy road. As I stepped outside the car, every fiber of my being went on alert. My body was covered in tremors, and I heard my spirit guides loudly saying, "Oh no, girl. You are not!" Nausea overtook me, and I felt like I was going to get sick right there on the side of the road. I got back in the car and told my son we could not go in. As we drove away (my teenage son was clearly disappointed), I caught a glimpse of the woods. I intuitively knew there were more headstones in the forest and that if we went in there, we could potentially be harmed. A dark presence guarded the area towards the woods. As we made the drive out of there, I knew we averted something nasty. The nausea finally subsided about ten minutes later.

As a consolation prize, I then drove us to the next

haunted location: Pine Hill Cemetery, aka Blood Cemetery. Abel Blood is buried there, and legend had it that the hand carving on his stone would face, and at night, the hand would point down. Sadly, when we arrived at the cemetery, we found the hand had been previously vandalized and removed. However, we still got experience for my little investigator. We walked around the cemetery, which was very peaceful. I recorded myself asking if there was a child there, no response.

I asked, "Is Abel Blood here?"

The response was a long-suffering sigh. I did not hear it in real-time, but rather when we played the recording back.

I used to visit the most amazing witch and metaphysical store in Salem, New Hampshire, named Dragon's Keep. The owners, Greg and Sandria, have a wealth of knowledge and give kind but honest direction in anything you need to know. One day I was visiting for a book, and as I was talking to Greg. I was very distracted by a young man peeking out of the bathroom at me. He was in his late teens to early twenties. He had dark hair, appeared in nineties clothing, and had a wide grin. His name was either Josh or Jake, but it began with J. He passed off a heroin overdose in the bathroom. I kept trying to speak with Greg, but J kept distracting me. I asked Greg what the building space was before his shop. He recalled it was previously a yoga studio. Nope, I was not getting anything on that one. He then thought carefully and said that many years ago, it had housed alcohol and drug addiction groups. Bingo. That explained J's death. He was very shy and wanted to communicate on his terms.

A few months later, I returned to Dragon's Keep for a Witches' Roundtable- which I highly recommend. The Roundtable is a gathering where amazing metaphysical group discussions often run into the late night. That evening, I wore my Guns N Roses t-shirt in honor of J and made sure I told him when I arrived. Throughout the evening, I could see him peeking around the bathroom door. I tried to encourage him to join the group, as I felt many other spirits around. In fact, at one point, while Greg was speaking, what felt like a cat brushed up against my leg. I brushed it away, thinking there was a strange fur feeling on my leg. It came back. Greg was watching and mentioned that his beloved rabbit had passed on but was a main fixture in the shop during his lifetime. As I was leaving for the night, I said goodbye to the group. I said, "Bye, J!" and as I passed a shelf, a box came flying off. I apologized to Greg for knocking it off. He laughed and said I did not. The box was thrown at me as I had announced to J and the group that I was leaving. Years later, he would show up in a reading.

I had the pleasure of investigating an old meeting house in a nearby town in New England. I had never been there, nor was I aware of the history of it. I was just excited to be around like-minded people who were spiritually open. That previous morning, I had worked at a psychic fair event, so I was still dressed up and wearing high-heel boots. I planned to stay an hour or so and then leave when I felt uncomfortable or bored. Well, the spirit world had other plans for me, and I was not bored. When I arrived, the local paranormal investigation crew greeted me and invited me to do a walk-through before they started. When I am entering a spiritually active location, I am often pulled with a magnetic force to go towards the spirit activity. It does not matter if it is a home, business, or graveyard. I must go to where I am directed. It is unavoidable, or the pull and physical sensations will not let up and sometimes become painful. At the meeting house, I was drawn to go upstairs. As I walked up the creaky and extremely narrow width stairs, I immediately regretted my choice of footwear since the town's early settlers obviously had tiny feet. My shoes barely fit on the stairs. When I reached the top floor, I was drawn to a box pew with the number 9 in it. I honestly cannot remember the rest of the number. My heart started to pound, and I felt panicky. I was drawn to look over the railing at the downstairs gallery. I had the vision that someone had gone over that railing. They were either pushed or fell, and I was apprehensive to get too close myself. I walked around to the other side and sat down. I got the impression that the family that sat in that box was an older couple- in their sixties. Young in this timeline but considered older in those days. I glanced around the room and then looked down at the undeveloped area in the gallery.

As I tuned into the energy, I immediately heard yelling, "There's a witch among us!"

At first, I thought the spirit world was referring to me, and I put a finger at myself and said, "Are you talking about me?" I was overcome with such a sense of fear and dread that I went back downstairs. I shared with the lead investigator what I got.

He said, "You don't know the history here, do you?"

I shook my head. He informed me that the meeting house was where Goody Cole was originally accused and tried of witchcraft, which now made sense as to why those impressions were so strong.

Another member of the team asked me to investigate a compartment area under the pulpit of the meeting house. I had an awful feeling when I was on the pulpit, and no, it is not because I am a witch. I felt such oppression, anger, and misuse of authority in the top pulpit area. Under the bottom pulpit area, I opened the door and saw the spirit of a Black man in the corner of the crawlspace, pointing to an area further in. I was not going in because 1) I hate confined spaces and 2) spiders, mice, and snakes. I shared about the gentleman I saw. The team later shared that the building was used as part of the Underground Railroad.

Later, the participants of the group showed up and seated themselves around in the meeting boxes. I was chatting with the medium who was participating in the night investigation.

I stood to stretch my legs, listening on and off to the team discuss various paranormal events, such as aliens and Bigfoot. I will be honest- I have zero interest in alien/UFO things. I also know I am going to be completely out of luck when they land because I did not pay attention all these years to people aware. I digress. I listened to the speakers, and suddenly, I heard heavy breathing in my right ear. I stopped and walked a bit over to where there were kids. I was thinking it was them. Asthmatic. Nope. I must note that they were extremely quiet and considerate kiddos. Okay, not them. I walked back to where I had been standing. The doors in the meeting boxes would open and close on their own. The participants kept talking but their eyes were getting larger as they looked at each other. To my right, the breathing started up again, but this time it was on my neck. I felt a male presence. My body was completely covered in chills and sweat. The temperature must have been about 50 degrees in the meeting house and dropping quickly. I excused myself and stepped outside to get some air and a light coat from my car. The other medium was walking out as well to retrieve something from her car. As soon as I stepped outside, I realized it was at least 70 degrees. Soaked in sweat and chills, I said goodbye to the other medium. I had no interest in hanging out with the Creepy Breather anymore that night.

She waved goodbye as I pulled out and yelled, "Ground and shower, girl!"

When I went to bed later that night, my blouse was still

soaked with sweat.

Haunted locations are nothing new to me. When my husband and I were searching for our first home, we visited many homes. Usually, I would not get anything from the homes except an imprint of those who lived there with their energy. Overall, it was an interesting experience. I always loved visiting other people's homes. I enjoyed seeing how they decorated and especially the energies they imprinted in the home. To quote my mother, "You can always tell whether a home is warm or cold." Most of the homes we visited had a warm vibe. However, one did not. My husband was so excited, as this home had a plush mancave in the basement. The home is in a newer neighborhood, very sought after. It was near my work- less than five minutes' drive and close to my husband's commute. The price of the home was exactly in our range. It seemed perfect. I started to go into the kitchen area and felt a little off, like a shift in time and space. Although the kitchen was not outdated at the time, darkness and it seemed outdated. It appeared to me to be a kitchen than what was physically in there. It did not go away even after we turned on the lights. We walked over to the staircase. I started up the stairs, and as I went up five stairs, it felt like I was walking through an immensely thick and humid wall. Nausea overtook me. I felt a horrible sense of dread, and whoever it was would not let me up the stairs. My husband went upstairs and checked it out while I excused myself outside. The sickening feeling did not leave until we were gone from the home. I later shared the story with one of my co-workers. She stated that there was a mysterious death of a woman on that street, and she thought that was the home. The husband had been a suspect. He was cleared of any charges but moved away shortly after that. After my experience, there was no doubt in my mind that the woman was still in the home. At that time, I could not wait to get the hell out of there. I often think of her and send her thanks for trying to protect me.

Chapter 4
The Lure Of New Orleans

New Orleans is a deeply spiritual place with an under-brooding sense of darkness tethered by light to keep the balance. If you ever needed a physical representation of heaven and hell, it is New Orleans. The poverty level is extreme, and there is a quest for survival. There is gang and drug violence. There is a supernatural current that makes you think there might be some truth to the stories about missing tourists, unusual encounters to with what they describe as vampires and experiences out on the mystical bayou at night. To offer balance, there is an air of mystery, excitement, and hope as soon as you enter the city as soon as you enter the airport after landing. New Orleans residents are survivors, and they do not give up easily. That drive and passion for the home they love is evident in the music, the food, and the people. I mean, where else would you be greeted by a jazz band as soon as you get off your flight? I have many cities I claim as home: Salem, Kansas City, but I will forever include NOLA as my city, which goes beyond the sense of wanderlust belonging. I have a strong family lineage there, but it is not my story to tell at this point here, with respect to the spirit world. I do want to mention my cousin K-, without you, I would not have found the bloodline. Blood always finds blood, and thank you.

I passed the Superdome several times during my travels

in and out of the city. There are no words to describe that feeling of knowing what occurred there during Katrina. It is a feeling of horror that I rarely experience, even with the dead. Some monsters are real. I want anyone who is connected to Katrina to know I keep you in my prayers- the victims, the emergency responders, dispatch, and everyone else connected with the tragedy that unfolded that day and in the aftermath. The city is healing and will continue to heal, but we will never ever forget.

New Orleans has a pulse, like NYC, but not quite. It is full of despair, sorrow, and hope. Once you get the city in your blood, it is difficult to let it go. You either love it or not. I am in love with the Big Easy, but not just the city itself. I am in love with the people, the spirits, the buildings, and the food. Every ounce of my blood became addicted to the energy of the Quarter. I craved the Creole and Cajun food. Nothing else would do while I was there. Others describe their spiritual awakening in NOLA. It goes beyond that. New Orleans changes you for the rest of your life, and it becomes part of your DNA, the good, the bad, and the ugly. I craved New Orleans, and I still do.

I traveled to NOLA about a year ago to connect with the land and my roots. I also coordinated clients and business meetings to make the most out of my time there. I checked into the Pontchartrain Hotel, which was quite an experience. The energy there is unmatched. The best way to describe the décor is something you would see out of a movie. As an original apartment building in the twenties, the hotel maintained the hotel décor. For me, as soon as I stepped into the lobby, my whole body started buzzing and tingling. It reminded me a little of the American Horror Story hotel but in a wonderful way. I immediately had to start wandering around the lobby, with its connecting bars, restaurant, and sitting rooms. I had not even gotten to my room yet, so I was dragging my suitcases along on this exploratory journey. I finally made my way to the fifth floor. I knew the other hotel floors had a reputation for being haunted, but I assumed my room would be fine.

I opened the door and was immediately taken in by the beauty of the room. It reminded me both in décor and psychic senses of someone's current, beautifully decorated apartment. I brought my suitcase in, and psychically, I felt like I was a guest in someone's apartment rather than a hotel room. I felt a woman's presence over by the chair in the bedroom. I ignored her and went to check the bathroom out. It was clean and well organized, within the original tile-style shower and flooring of the 1930s/40s. The antique wooden medicine cabinet held antique pharmaceutical bottles with the original prescription labels and names from the 1800s and 1900s. As I read the labels, I realized there was someone watching me in the bathroom, close to the window. As I walked out of the bathroom, I laid the ground rules.

"You and I can talk, but when it is bedtime, which it is. It is my time."

The woman seemed to listen but still had some antics up her spirit sleeves.

When I originally booked the hotel room, I specifically requested a view of the beloved city. I was excited about my anticipated view and walked over to the huge window area. As I went over to pull the curtains back, two hands grabbed the back of my calf muscles. It felt like both muscles seizing up, that was how strong the intensity was. I stepped back and walked over to the window. It happened again. At this point, I breathed deeply and tried to let it go. The view was breathtaking at dusk and even more so at night. I went to dinner and later had a few phone calls for reading. I came back and went into the bathroom to prepare for a night in. As I walked over to the shower, the door opened on its own. Without fail, every time I closed the door, it slowly opened. I figured it was an air conditioning draft, so I put a towel behind the door to prop it closed. I wanted to keep the bathroom light on overnight, but not shining in full blast to keep me awake. Tired from travel, I lay down in the luxurious, huge bed and started to doze off. I felt someone sitting on the other side of the spacious bed, as the weight shifted and there was a slight pull on the down-light blanket. My eyes popped open. I wound up falling asleep again with the light on and fully dressed. I made sure my crystal bracelets and necklaces were on. I woke up around one in the morning and got up to use the bathroom. The bathroom door was wide open, and the towel I had placed behind the door looked as if it had been completely removed. I was more annoyed at this point than frightened, but I did move the towel back and went back to sleep. As my alarm went off the next morning at 6 am, I woke up and reached over to turn it off.

As I started to pull back the covers, I heard a woman whisper in my right ear, "Sorry!"

I took a moment to catch my breath and said, "You should be. This bed is for me only."

I took a quick shower and walked over to the window to see what the weather was like. I felt the same sensation of two hands grabbing me on the back of my legs. At that point, I had enough. "You need to stop! I need to see whether it is raining or not, and how I need to dress today! Now stop it! This window is sealed." I tapped the windowsill. "I'm not going to jump out or fall."

She complied and finally let me go to the window without grabbing me. However, the bathroom was not negotiable, and the door continued to open no matter how many tricks I tried. I finally consented to that one.

After a delicious breakfast and some people watching at Whistle Stop Café, I left New Orleans and drove out to Vacherie, to check out Oak Valley Plantation. I had to pass over Hale Boggs Bridge to get there, and I hate bridges. I cannot describe why, as I feel like it is something connected to a transition to the afterlife. I did labor breathing exercises as I passed over the Hale Boggs and moved into the parishes. The immense peace I felt while driving was unlike anything else. Like I was home. I will have to say it was isolated out there. I passed the Bayou outlets and marveled at the moving gators in the water, with people fishing right in front of them off the road. I had the air conditioning off, as it was a beautiful day. It had just finished raining, so I put the window down. As I passed a certain point in the road past the second bayou outlet, my entire body was covered with chills. Covered head to toe, it was a sensation of fight or flight, like how a body reacts to a tiger chasing it. I could not figure out what was happening. I never reacted like that except when a spirit was being nasty, and I was feeling threatened. I breathed through it, and the sensation eased up and finally released.

The Oak Valley Plantation was beautiful but mostly uneventful. I chose not to do the tour of the Big House, due to its being cheap, and I did not want to be with other tourists. I just wanted to walk around to connect outside. It started raining again. Carrying my umbrella, I walked through the cabin paths of the enslaved. I stopped at one and put my umbrella down. There was a woman spirit still taking care of her sick kids. It felt residual, but I did speak and let her know I saw her. I moved into another building where the slaves' names were painted on the wall. A female tourist went over to the wall, pointed to a name, and said, "Quick, take my picture! I found my name!" as if it were a name keychain in a gift shop. She posed for a picture pointing to the wall. I was hoping above that a spirit would smack her on the back of her head. She left the cabin. A tall Black man and I were now the only two in there. We looked at each other and both shook our heads at the idiot woman. He was tall with a larger football player build. He had glasses and short hair. We both went over to the glass cabinet. As we read the pharmacy roster for the plantation slaves, we touched the glass at the same time as we leaned over. As we were still reading, a strange pulse went through me and him at the same time. We both said, "Whoa!" looked at each other, and quickly exited the cabin. We continued to look through the buildings and read the historical recounts of the plantation. I noticed he did not go into the Big House either.

I ate lunch out at the plantation and drove back. I wanted to get down to the Quarter. During my trip back to the hotel, I was planning and organizing numerous things in my head due to being short on time. Again, the same thing happened with full-body chills when I hit a certain point. At this point, I knew something from the other side was happening, so I made a mental note of the location, "Fashion Plantation." I safely got across the bridge and back to the hotel. I googled Fashion. It was a newly built housing development on what was the original location of a plantation. I called my dad, who said, "Oh yes. That is your body's response to pure evil. It sounds like something horrific happened there. You should go back and check it out!"

"Thanks, Dad."

I quickly got ready to head down to the French Quarter I had dinner reservations and clients that night, so I was on a time crunch. I boarded the streetcar to head down to the Quarter. Well, there is more backstory to getting on the streetcar. After many conversations, encouragement, and map reviews with the amazing parking valets at Pontchartrain, I boarded the streetcar.

The conversation did include me saying, "Seriously if I get lost or stuck, $200 is yours. You get me in my car. No questions asked."

They laughed and watched me across the street as I boarded. I felt confident as I took my seat until I saw one of them make the sign of the cross.

My plan was to head down to Bourbon Street. Without much ado, the car made its way to the Quarter. When the prompt screen announced we were at the scheduled stop, I started to get up. My spirit guides said, "No, you are not. You are going to Jackson."

Now, at this point in my life at forty-six years old, I have learned that I no longer argue with the dead or my guides. Many times, those spirits have kept me alive by listening.

An older couple from Maryland (I had eavesdropped on their conversation) was seated across from me. I asked them where they were headed.

The man replied, "Jackson Square."

I replied, "Huh. So am I."

The car continued onto the French Market stop, and I saw my spirit guide sit back and cross her arms in an empty seat, satisfied. The couple got off, and I followed closely behind. When I looked up, I saw I was on Decatur Street, and I knew I was home, having become familiar with the street. I popped into the cutest shop based on name alone Sassy Magick. I wandered in, and a woman offered me a reading. I declined and stated I was also a reader but short on time due to pressing commitments. Note to reader- if you can do a reading there, do it! We chatted, and she asked where I was from. I told her I lived in New Hampshire but had connections to Massachusetts and Salem. She asked if I were a witch, and I confirmed, replying that I was a Cabot witch and a member of the Temple. "So is his husband!" pointing to the man behind the counter.

"No way!" I excitedly made my way over to him. He and I chatted, and he helped me look for a new tarot deck. I cannot for the life of me remember the name, but I know exactly what he looked like and how his energy felt. Talk about a good vibe! I bought a good money wash soap. I do have to mention they have an awesome supply of books as well, but my dear husband only said I needed one large suitcase for my three-day trip!

I popped into Omen, which is also an amazing shop. The connectivity to the pulse of magick and ancestral voodoo and hoodoo magick is unparalleled. The shop clerks were pleasant and helpful, and they were excited to talk about Salem! I grabbed some magickal supplies I needed (again, this is your place to go for the real deal) and checked them out. That was an hour in total. I headed into a courtyard that came out to the open-air market, and that was it. I remember listening to music and walking around. I talked with people, and I think at one point, I grabbed a gluten-free beignet from the market. When I looked at my watch, it declared that I had been down in the Quarter for almost three and a half hours. I missed a business meeting on the next street over, missed a phone call from a local friend, and I honestly cannot tell you how I lost track of time. It is like time freezes when you are down there, or rather, you cannot recount what you just did during that time.

I did not want to be down in the Quarter at night, by myself. I got on the streetcar and headed back towards the hotel. As we made our way towards the other end of town, a man entered the car. He did not pay, and he was having what I would call a moment as he sat down in the middle of the floor. The streetcar proceeded.

Suddenly, I heard, "Get off now!"

I pulled the cord and signaled that I wanted the next stop. Another woman jumped off with me as well. I started to walk. Great. I was at least a good mile from my hotel in

NOLA by myself. And the sun was starting to fade. This beautiful Black woman spirit with a large chignon like the one Marie Leveau used to wear appears next to me in the doorway of one of the shops. I took a deep breath, and suddenly, a thin Black man with a baseball cap and blue backpack showed up right in front of me. I still do not know where he came from.

She pointed to him and said to me, "Stay with him, and don't leave until he does."

Heeding the warning, I stayed close behind him. Once we reached this tattoo shop close to the hotel, he vanished into thin air. I went into the shop, almost drawn there. Much to my delight, NOLA PD was already in there taking a report for something. Now, a side note- I absolutely adore Louisiana law enforcement, as I have worked on a few missing and cold cases in the state for them. NOLA PD is unlike anything else in my book. Heart emoji. The presence of the PD in the city is not just a reassurance; it is a complete immersion into the community as one. So, a huge thank you to the people of the NOLA PD for all you do.

I was three doors away from my hotel. I made it back, much to the delight and concern of the valets. They were happy I was back in one piece but more concerned I did not get off the streetcar and walked. I had dinner, read for clients, and played the bathroom game with my spirit roommate. The next day, it was time to return home to New England. I did not want to get on the flight. I knew I belonged back down

South, and I needed to be closer to New Orleans. In fact, every time we looked at potential places to live, I would ask, "How far is that for NOLA?" At that exact time, my husband had been awaiting transfer orders to Florida.

Still at the hotel, I text him and say, "I'm not coming home unless we are moving south."

He texts me back, "Get on flight. I got the orders!"

As I was packing my bag, I remembered a friend told me to grab dirt from the city before I left. I had packed a little glass vial just for that purpose. I went out in front of the hotel, squatted down in the grass, and got my dirt. As I was banging it in the bottle to settle, NOLA PD rolled up, watched what I was doing, smiled, and drove on. I walked back to the hotel front, where the valets were watching.

"You'll be back, baby."

Chapter 5
Reach Out And Touch Someone

When I connect with the spirit world, it is most often through my third eye. It is a similar feeling to watching a movie in a theater, except that the theater is sitting or standing right by me. It is rarer to have spirits materialize to the point it is a living person. However, that rare event recently happened two times in one month.

I had not been able to see spirit materialize since I was about twenty years old. It started up again with the loss of my husband's grandfather. I had always had a strong connection to my husband's grandfather, Papa. He was a proud United States Marine. As I am writing this, I checked in with him to see if it is okay. I hear his strong Boston accent.

"Yeah, yes. That is fine."

Papa served in World Two and was a true pillar of strength for my husband during his youth. At Papa's viewing right before the funeral, I was in the bathroom crying.

My husband called out, "Court, we need to go!"

I made a face and did not budge. I did not want to leave Papa. I clearly heard Papa's thick Boston accent in that bathroom, "Jesus Christ. You are going to make me late for my own funeral!"

I was so shocked that I started laughing and finally left the bathroom to make it to his funeral on time.

About a month or so after he passed, my husband was riding bikes with our sons in our driveway at our old home in Virginia. I looked out the window and saw my husband talking to an older man. He was standing close next to my husband in the driveway. My husband was straddling his bike- the other man was so close to him he could touch him if he wanted to. The elderly man was wearing khaki pants, a white shirt, sneakers, and an old newsie cap. My husband and he were laughing. I remember thinking that the older man was out walking and saw my husband, thinking he was military (short haircut), he stopped to make conversation. I also thought it was strange because our neighborhood was so spread out, that people did not often stop and talk. When I opened the door to tell my husband that I did not want the boys that far up the driveway, I realized who the older man was. It was Papa. I screamed my husband's name, and when I looked back, Papa was gone. The stop sign that sat across the street was now visible. The appearance had been so strong that he had blocked out the stop sign across the street. For a large part of my marriage, I had never shared with my husband that I could see spirits. The only thing he knew about my gifts was that I often knew things and we had connections in Salem.

That night, we were sitting on the couch, and Chris said, "You know, I was thinking about my grandfather today."

And that is when I told him about my abilities.

The next time I saw spirit in person was many years later. I was an educator at several elementary schools. Most I absolutely loved. This was not one of them, and the feeling was mutual. That Wednesday, I had plans to be at another building but needed to catch up on work at this one. Two staff members needed my room for a meeting, so I left and felt the need to go down to the staff mailboxes. I entered the lounge and saw a large woman sitting down at a table in front of the boxes with her cane placed next to her. I said hello and carefully squeezed past the woman, cautious not to bump her cane. I was proud of my agility due to the tight spacing. Now, I am not someone who can just not say something if there is another person in my space. Moments of silence are torture for me.

I turned to her and jokingly said, "I'm looking to see if they finally put my name on the box."

They finally had, and I turned to say that to her. She opened her mouth and made a strange "Ahhhhh" sound as if she were trying to communicate but could not, as if she were choking on her words. I thought she had been impacted by a previous stroke due to her facial movement and speech patterns. I said goodbye and walked out. As I made my way down the hall, I thought it was rude of me not to introduce myself and my position, but I shrugged and kept walking. I did not think about her until a week later when a staff email went out. The secretary announced a building member had passed the previous Wednesday morning. She had been homebound for weeks with a critical illness. I was curious, so I looked her up on Facebook. It was the woman in front of the mailboxes who would have either been already crossed or crossing when she appeared to me. I did what any normal person would do, medium or not. I freaked out and called my dad. He advised me to try to connect with her spirit again, as he felt she had a message. I never connected again with her, although I tried once more.

A month later, I was working at an event. I had blocked off a lunch break for myself when I heard a woman's voice at the door, food still in hand. She was very distraught and said she was having a difficult day. I told her to sit down, and I shut the door behind her. She did not offer or motion to close it herself. She shared that she was severely depressed and was thinking of ending her life. I immediately stopped eating and talked with her more. She begged me to do the reading, even though I knew others were waiting after my break. She was very distraught and said some alarming but unusual things. I wanted to stop reading and refer her. She insisted I had to do the reading. I set the timer. She shared how depressed she had been about her marriage and her husband. I noticed she kept referring to them in the past. "My kids were 16, I would have been 35, etc." At the conclusion of the truly short reading (10-15 minutes), I offered her my card and begged her to please reach out for help from a professional counselor. I even offered to sit with her while she made the call, which she declined. I thought it was odd she did not touch the card. I stood up with her, and she waited for me to open the door. She walked out, and I thought it was odd that she went down the hallway and seemed to disappear, as it was a dead end. The other doors for event vendors were closed. I shrugged, as it had been a long day already and I noticed the next client had been sitting, waiting patiently outside the door. I excused myself, and I ran to find the host of the event to inform her about the statements the client had made in case we needed to call mental health help. The proprietor checked the entire area, as well as the other staff members but had no recollection of this woman. It was as if she did not exist.

At this point, I was running way behind. I invited the next lady in. She noted that she did not want to interrupt my break, as she knew I needed to eat. I laughed and shared that I had read for that client and that I would eat later. She seemed confused and said that she did not see anyone go in or come out. The reading continued, but I could not shake that odd feeling. When I cashed out that evening, my sign-in sheet matched exactly minus one, her. I shrugged it off and was ready to go home. It was not until I was in the shower that night that I realized that a spirit had materialized. Again, a phone call to Dad.

The spirit world wants and often demands to be heard. Think of it as someone who moves out of state. Even though they no longer live in the same state as you, they still want to be a part of your life. They still want to communicate with you, even if it cannot be in person. That is what meditation and opening your ears and eyes to the spirit world is for. One of the best ways to communicate with them is to just be. Be silent, be open, be ready to see. They will find a way to reach you when they need to.

When we first moved to New Hampshire, I searched for an area to run in. I found it at our local cemetery. Forest Hills houses the remains of over 10,000 people. It dates to the 1700s. Needless to say, it is for me to walk and run and a community within the spirit world. One day, a small hand took mine. The spirit child was about three or four. I walked along, holding the child's hand. It guided me over to a grave. I was confused as to why I was led there. I noticed the grave was a Marine lost in combat during Vietnam. His grave marker with the Marine flag was askew. I walked and straightened it out. The child took my hand once again, and as we walked a little further- I assured the child that they were loved and could move onto heaven. There would be someone to take care of them. The child's hand released, and I knew I was alone again.

My oldest son shares my gifts, although he has pushed them away as he has gotten older. When he was about 13 months old, I took him with me on a local ghost tour of Fredericksburg. I went with a group of neighbors. As we got to the St George cemetery, my son was beyond excited. He gestured to get out of his stroller so he could see better. The neighbor held him, and he was waving and laughing in the dark cemetery as if there were an entire party going on. The tour guide was a real pill, and became annoyed at his laughter.

When he was a toddler, we would go to events at Loriella Park in Virginia. I was remarkably familiar with it since I had grown up playing tennis there. The park housed a playground, tennis courts, soccer fields, and the original Loriella family house, which became the Parks and Recreation building. We were playing on the playground when he wandered away from the other kids. I followed him. He was on a mission as he kept towards the back woods. He stopped at an area that had a tiny broken metal fence around, like a garden. He walked into the sectioned-off area and started chattering and laughing like he was dancing with friends. I laughed and asked him with whom he was playing. I glanced at the side of the area and noticed a nondescript plaque that noted this was the resting place of the enslaved, with no markers, names, or stones. Every time we visited the playground, my son made it a point to visit it.

When I was about ten, we moved to Virginia. My parents and their visiting friends would tour all the colonial Fredericksburg sites. I would get dragged along and be bored. The only redeeming quality was Caroline Square, an antique store. I would go upstairs to the attic and basement sections of the stores and play for hours, entertained by the spirits hanging around their old items. My favorite spirit was a woman from the 1950s who would hang around her furs. She was very glamorous. Twenty years later, when my oldest son was three, I took him to the store I played in the most. This was his first visit there. My dear friend Heather had purchased it. My son asked me to go upstairs and play with the fire trucks. I was okay with that, but I told him there probably were no toys up there. It was all antiques, and Heather had a special stash of toys and treats downstairs that she let him have. He repeated his request, so I took him upstairs. He carefully held onto the railing and climbed the steps. He walked with purpose to the very back of the upstairs section. Hidden underneath a table with a long cloth were two enormous fire trucks. We came downstairs with one, and Heather asked how he knew they were there.

He said, "They told me!"

My son's connection with the spirit world did not end there. When my oldest son was five, he participated in a fun run race at his school. It was a hard year- the school was not a good match for him. The teacher was not patient. He was nervous about it, especially with the large crowd. My Mom and I went to watch him. At the start of the race, a little girl wearing sneakers, a denim skirt, and a red top with spaghetti straps loudly took his hand and said, "Come on, D-!" My Mom and I were thrilled that he had a friend. They ran the first lap holding hands, and then suddenly, she was gone. He ran over twenty-nine out of thirty-two laps in that race. I asked my son who the girl was. He said he did not know her.

I later asked the teacher via email who she was. She checked with the other teachers. They had no idea who we were describing, as all the students in the race had white-issued T-shirts, and no one matched that description.

We have moved quite a bit over the years, and I swear many a paranormal event started, "We were just trying to get to know the new area." I spend so much time in the spirit world that I often forget others do not. My family and I decided to journey to a haunted old jail in Florida. As we entered the famous old, haunted jail, I felt strangely calm. My friend had previously visited here a month earlier and warned me to load up on my energy shields and crystal protections. I was sure glad I listened that day! Our tour guide was an adorable twenties something, who did an amazing job staying in character as an inmate but also balanced the drama with insightful and accurate information. We entered the jail cell, and the guide instructed the women to enter the cells that were designated for the female inmates. We did, and I felt nothing. He then directed us towards another group of cells around the corner. I started to feel panicky, and I knew there was something amiss. All my senses started buzzing as they did when a spirit was near and trying to get attention. Out of the corner of my eye, I saw a spirit in the form of a very tall man standing in the cell to the right of me. He was leaning against the cell bed, arm propped on the railing.

I said to my husband, "Something's not right in here."

My husband said, "Oh, here we go. Do not say anything!"

The guide (ever in tune with the group) said, "Why? You get bad vibes in here?"

"Yes, well actually I'm a psychic medium."

Everyone else in the group looked at me like I had three heads, which they were waiting to spin around.

The guide replied, "OH! Let me know what you get?" I nodded and continued his talk.

"Well, folks. This here is solitary confinement."

He relayed which type of offenders would be housed there If you look at this picture here, you will see this man (he said his name, but I am not bringing that energy into the book)." He continued to tell the story that the man shot his wife's lover and was scheduled to be hanged that day. A woman in the tour group asked if the inmate was in the picture.

The guide tapped the man in the middle of the photograph and said, "That is him. He is waiting to be hung."

He cracked a joke, and I felt a huge whoosh blow past me.

The guide started to speak again and grabbed his throat. He cleared it a few times, then excused himself.

"I am sorry guys. I am not feeling so well. I am going to step over here and y'all look around."

At that point, I knew what had happened. The spirit had grabbed him.

My husband glared at me. "What did you do to him?'

"Oh, stop. It was not me this time."

I went over to the guide, who was extremely pale.

"Are you okay?" I asked him, my concern growing.

"Yeah, I feel like I'm going to throw up and my throat feels funny."

I nodded my head. "That is them grabbing you. Just release   it."
I proceeded to the rest of the tour with my family but noticed the guide was gone. After we were done, I told my husband and kids I was going to check on the guide, who I saw outside   the   building   drinking   water.

"I'm going to check on him!" My husband nodded and murmured to our kids, "Can't take her anywhere."

The kids agreed and decided to go look at gator heads. I walked over to the guide.

"Are you okay?"

"Yeah. That is weird, that has never happened to me. What was that?"

"Well, you will need to ground yourself and set some boundaries. You obviously must go back there since it is your job. Next time, say, "This is not acceptable. And for

God's sake, do not crack that joke again."

"Does that ever happen to you?"

"All the time! I have been choked, scratched, pinched, shocked. The nausea, headaches, and chest pressure are the worst."

"That sounds horrible!"

"Oh, it is! But that is just the spirit world trying to communicate." I smiled, and we said goodbye.

After we moved to Florida, my family and I visited the Ximinez Fatio house on several occasions. The first time, I went with my two sons. We stumbled upon the house by accident. We originally were supposed to visit the military hospital museum, but the tour guide explained that it was more auditory than visual. He clearly knew we were a visual family, so we thanked him and left. As we left the building and turned onto the street, I was drawn to go left. It was a magnetic pull. The boys followed, and we stopped in front of the Ximinez house. I said, "We must go in here. Now."

"Why?" they asked.

"I don't know, but I have to."

They sighed, but they followed me as we went into the gift shop to get tickets. The shop clerk greeted us and handed us little handheld black devices to hold. It reminded me of one of the original cell phones, large but easy to carry. These devices would give us a recorded tour that matched the room we were in. We took the self-guided tour, and within two rooms, my youngest decided to venture off on his own. I did not mind, as we were the only people in the house at the time. I figured, what could he get into? It was an hour before closing, and we had just enough time to get through the house. My oldest and I were in the dining room, listening to the tour and checking out the historic furniture.

My son ran to us and yelled, "Mommy, mommy! Someone touched me!"

"Who? Where?"

"No. Not like that. Just- come on. Come."

My other son and I followed him upstairs and headed to another set of stairs.

"Are you even supposed to be up here?"

"Yes, Mom."

We went into the attic area. I started to feel buzzing in my body, and my left hand started to tingle. I could feel the electricity in the air. "I was just standing here, Mom. I was looking at this guy" (pointed to the picture on the wall) "and he touched me on my back!"

The photo of the man was of a Black man in a military uniform, with shiny buttons on his uniform, and he was holding a musket beside him. Underneath the photo, the caption read "Bugle Boy."

I assured my son that if someone from the spirit world touched him, they would try to communicate. I tapped into the man's energy and felt a sense of protection and calm.

My son nodded his head.

"He's a soldier, like me. My son is thirteen and absolutely loves everything connected to the military, particularly wars starting with World War Two and working backward. He is an old soul."

I let the kids explore the room, and I quickly realized what the attic was when I saw the bedding on the floor. It was the servants' room. Not quarters. It was a tiny attic room. It had to be one hundred degrees outside that day, and upstairs in the non-air-conditioned house… it made me nauseous to think of the living conditions. The boys started to head back downstairs. I looked at the other photos of the other former slaves on the wall. As I looked at the people, I zeroed in on a woman close to the Bugle Boy. The caption under the photo read, "Escaped from Louisiana." I stood for a few more minutes and said goodbye. It is important to note that when I originally wrote this paragraph, I worded her section differently as "fled" and "path to freedom." As I hit the period key, the passage was deleted. I respected the spirit woman and rewrote the passage.

I hope you have enjoyed my journey so far! My hope is that you gained a greater understanding of what it is like to be a witch and psychic medium. If you are the parent of a child with budding gifts, please support them in any way you can. Let them know they are special and not alone. They were chosen for a reason. The world is more open to accepting the unexplained. Embrace it and them!